D0118702

GIZMO

BARRY VARELA   Illustrations by **ED BRIANT**

A NEAL PORTER BOOK
ROARING BROOK PRESS
NEW MILFORD, CONNECTICUT

For N and P
—B.V.

For Diane
—E.B.

A Neal Porter Book
Published by Roaring Brook Press
Roaring Brook Press is a division of Holtzbrinck Publishing Holdings Limited Partnership
143 West Street, New Milford, Connecticut 06776

Distributed in Canada by H. B. Fenn and Company, Ltd.

Library of Congress Cataloging-in-Publication Data
Varela, Barry.
Gizmo / Barry Varela. — 1st ed.
p. cm. "A Neal Porter book."
Summary: When Professor Ludwig von Glink's contraption gets so out of hand that the City Buildings and
Permits Inspector condemns his home, the City Contemporary Art Museum comes to the rescue.
ISBN-13: 978-1-59643-115-7   ISBN-10: 1-59643-115-6
[1. Machinery—Fiction.   2. Stories in rhyme.]   I. Title.
PZ8.3.V712527Gi 2007   [Fic]—dc22   2006012007

Roaring Brook Press books are available for special promotions and premiums.
For details, contact: Director of Special Markets, Holtzbrinck Publishers.

Printed in China
First Edition April 2007
10 9 8 7 6 5 4 3 2 1

Professor Ludwig von Glink's
contraption started out
as little more than a vague notion
concerning perpetual motion.
The good professor woke up one fine spring morning
convinced that a particular arrangement of pulleys,
pendulums, sprockets, and gears suspended
by a network of wires would produce movement
that never ended.

an umbrella and its accompanying umbra,
flywheels and catapults, and an unspecified number of
valves, nozzles, and coils,
clamps, fins, and foils,
a pump, a cleaver,
a cantilever,
an electric fan, a whirligig,
some kind of gadgety whatchamacallit thingamajig,
a spring and a sproing, a joint and a joist.

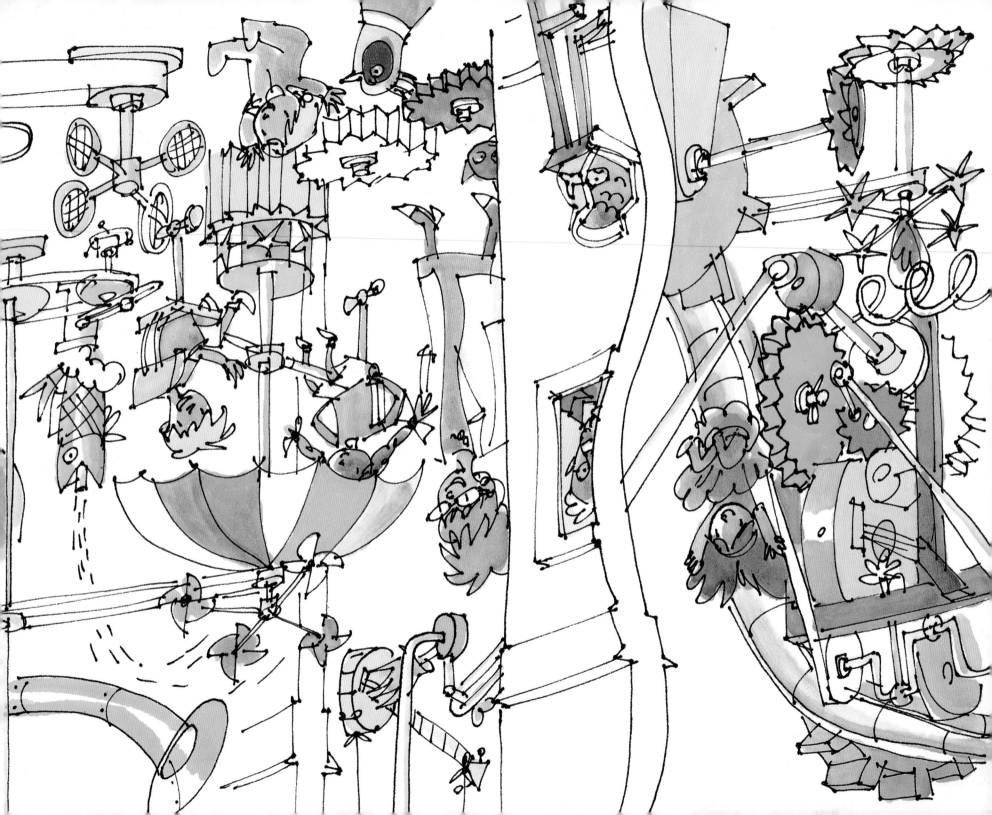

He was wrong.

The machine didn't move for long.
But before it ran out of steam,
his failed perpetual-motion machine
produced sounds of clanging and banging,
and pinging and ringing,
that were not entirely unpleasant,
as well as tingly, tangly twitterings
reminiscent of the call of the
ring-necked pheasant.
And the way in which
the device shimmied swervily,
and teetered topsy-turvily,
in a manner that was somehow
both lifelike and robotic,
was oddly hypnotic.

*What a wonderful, charming, enchanting
(he thought) Gizmo!
Not sure I'm sure exactly what it is, though.
In any case perhaps I ought,
just as an experiment,*

$$T^2(a+n)P\left(\frac{6}{7}\right)n \rightarrow$$
$$y\underline{a} = F(abcZ)HTe \rightarrow$$
$$F\pm\frac{(a)}{7}$$

To work up some specs
and see if I can make this
mingle-mangle of intricate
jury-rigged gimcrackery
yet more complex.
I'll bet dollars to doughnuts
that'd add to the merriment.

$$F = \mu n \rightarrow$$
$$y = mx + b$$

$$\dot{x}_i + V \rightarrow + \tfrac{1}{2}at^2 \quad Fe\tfrac{1}{2}K\Delta x^2$$

$$\eta t^{\rightarrow} + V_i'$$

$$V_i^2 + 2a\Delta x$$

$$F\Delta x \cos = \Delta$$

$$E_G = mph$$

$$Y - Y_P = m$$

$$(x - x_P)$$

$$a_c = \frac{V^2}{R}$$

$$Fc = \downarrow$$

$$F_6 \subset G\frac{m_c m_{R2}}{R^7}$$

$$Fe = K\frac{q_1 q_2}{RE}$$

$$\leq IN^3 \left(\frac{4ec}{K}\right)^K \leq IFc$$

$$\frac{100N}{7} \text{ and } K = Beg\frac{\infty}{4}$$

$$\left[C^5 + I\left(\frac{S+K}{S+I}\right)N^2\right]\left(\frac{Sm\log n^2}{S-1}\right)$$

$$K^5(S-1) \leq N^2 \; 23 + \log_N 2 \; (5+I)\left(\frac{C}{E}\right)$$

$$\left[\frac{2Ce^2(5+K)}{}\right]I \leq N3\left(\frac{4ec}{4}\right)$$

$$3 + I\left(\frac{3+K}{SH}\right)$$

$$+I \; e^3 \; C^3 \left(\frac{5H}{S-1}\right)^2 \left|\frac{\infty}{2}N \leq \right.$$

Ｆirst he attached a ball-peen hammer, which immediately contributed in a most satisfactory way to the clamor.

Next he fastened on ramps, slides,
buttons, lenses, switches,
notches and nodes,
nubbins and niches,

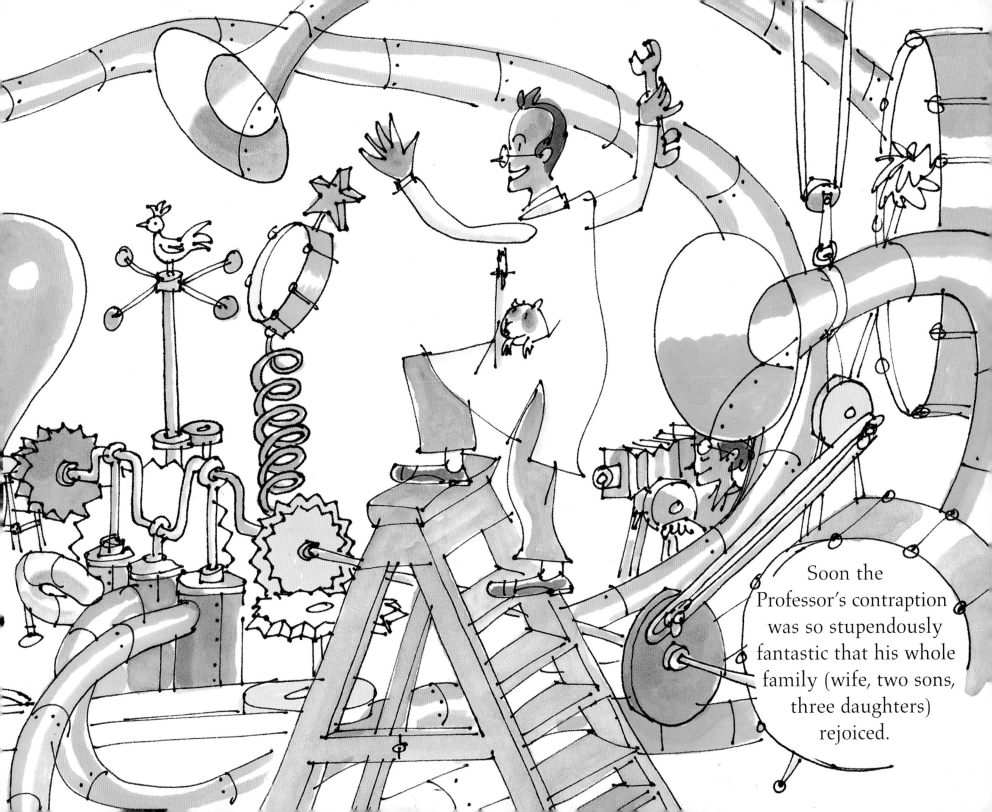

Soon the Professor's contraption was so stupendously fantastic that his whole family (wife, two sons, three daughters) rejoiced.

The structure grew and grew until it ran from the parlor up the stairs, into the attic,

and onto the roof, where it was topped with spokes and a giant propeller.

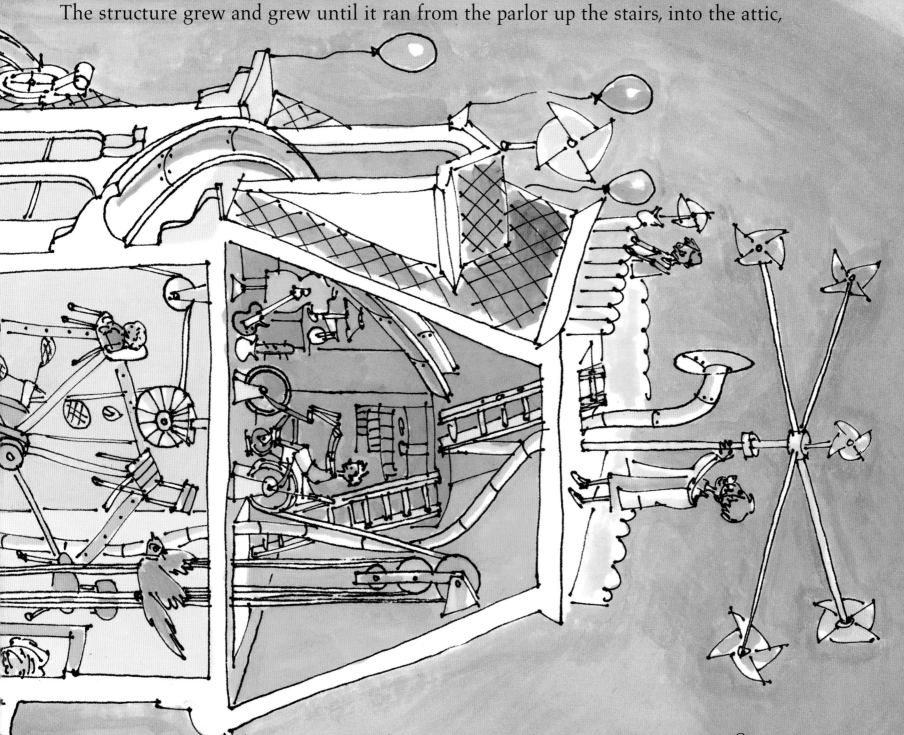

Then back down through the bedrooms it raced, into the kitchen, out the window.

Folks
came from far and near
to wonder and marvel
and listen and point
and gasp and laugh and cheer.

One day the City Buildings and Permits Inspector
arrived to measure every angle,
line,
curve,
and vector,
in order to verify that
the eccentric abode,
conformed in detail
to the city code.

Unfortunately, the Gizmo of Prof. L. von G.
had no function, utility, or practical purpose
he could see.
What did it do? Why was it made?
Did it have no use?

It couldn't possibly be there
simply to amuse!
The man didn't know what
to make of whimsy,

but he knew some other things:
The construction was
unorthodox,
the materials flimsy,
and worst of all there was no
"Form-S22: Permit for Addition
to Domicile or Dwelling,"
prominently displayed.

There was no telling
what other errors had been made.
Deeply offended by the pointless
contraption,
the Inspector concluded
that the whole kaboodle
must be on the verge
of collapsion.
Performing his duty
without dereliction,
he neither hawed
nor hemmed:

OFFICIAL NOTICE
OF EVICTION!

PROPERTY
CONDEMNED!

read the sign he tacked to the front door.
He left and was seen no more.

The von Glinks' beloved (if unusual) home, whose
every window was squeegeed, mantel dusted,
and doorknob polished,
was to be demolished.
Not to mention the fact that the Gizmo,
in all its twittering, flittering, whizzing,
whirring kinetic glory,
would go the way
of the dinosauri.

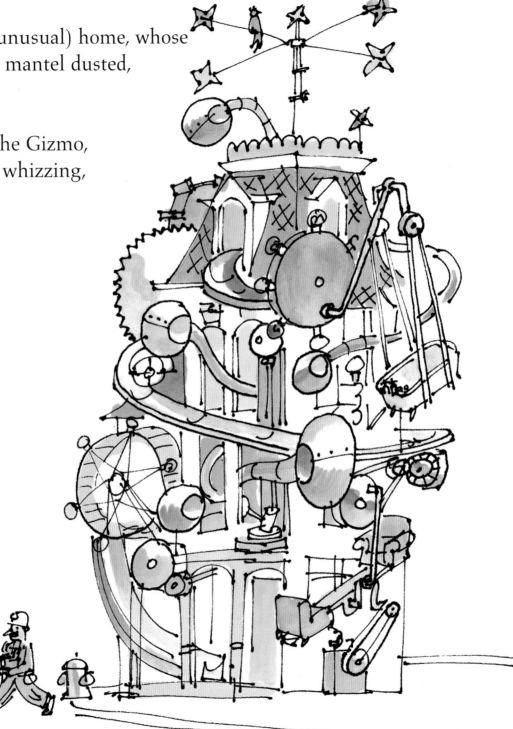

The demolition team arrived with a bulldozer,
a backhoe, and a dozen sticks of TNT.

They'd start knocking things down
the next day at three.

A reporter from the *Times-Herald-Post-Star-Sun*
got wind of the story.

Thus the article in the next morning's paper
(kindly turn to page 4E):

4E

POPULAR SCULPTURE TO BE DESTROYED

*A work of art enjoyed
By one and all
Will go under the wrecking ball
At three o'clock today.*

The Director of the City Contemporary Art Museum (CCAM)
slammed the paper down and shouted, "Not if I have anything to say about it!"

She called her friend the Mayor and demanded the house be
declared a landmark, a treasure, a historic site—
anything to save it from the dynamite.
The Mayor saw in the contraption,
a lucrative tourist attraction,
and she agreed:
The demolition must not proceed.

So after a close shave,
the Professor's Gizmo was saved.
Although any practical purpose it may have served
remained opaque:

She called her friend the Mayor and demanded the house be
declared a landmark, a treasure, a historic site—
anything to save it from the dynamite.
The Mayor saw in the contraption,
a lucrative tourist attraction,
and she agreed:
The demolition must not proceed.

So after a close shave,
the Professor's Gizmo was saved.
Although any practical purpose it may have served
remained opaque:

It was a case of art for art's sake.
And if by chance you're interested
in meeting the good
Professor,
all you have to do to see him

is stop by his office in the new Annex to
the City Contemporary Art Museum.